*To William*
*with thanks*

**Tosca's Christmas**
© Frances Lincoln Limited 1989
Text copyright © Matthew Sturgis 1989
Illustrations copyright © Anne Mortimer/Davan-Wetton Design

Tosca's Christmas was edited and designed by
Frances Lincoln Limited, Apollo Works,
5 Charlton Kings Road, London NW5 2SB
From an original concept by
Davan-Wetton Design

ISBN 0-7112-0568-X

9 8 7 6 5 4 3 2

Printed in Hong Kong by
Kwong Fat Offset Printing Co., Ltd

Design and art direction Debbie MacKinnon

# TOSCA'S CHRISTMAS

## ANNE MORTIMER
### STORY BY MATTHEW STURGIS

FRANCES LINCOLN

Tosca was enjoying a little nap. She was curled up amongst the cushions in a large armchair, dreaming of steamed haddock.

"You can't stay there, Tosca, we've got to move that chair."

Tosca padded upstairs to find a quiet corner. She was a cat who liked her naps. Perhaps there would be a bedroom door open. There was.

All over the bed there were toys, and a sea of bright coloured paper. What fun, thought Tosca, a paper chase. But before she could stretch her claws she was put out on to the landing.

"You can't come in here, Tosca. I'm doing my wrapping."

Tosca wondered what was happening. She was not used to being bossed about.

There was chaos downstairs. The hallway was full of prickly holly, the kitchen thick with interesting smells. There was a large, dark brown pudding on the kitchen table, and several mince pies . . .

"No, Tosca, you can't eat one of those."

Beside the fireplace where Tosca's armchair usually stood there was now a tall fir tree. They were all busy decorating it with glittering balls, bright streamers and coloured lights.

"Look at the Christmas tree, Tosca. Isn't Christmas exciting?"

Tosca was not excited. She sat under the tree and sulked. Tosca didn't like Christmas very much. Everyone was too busy enjoying themselves to think of her. And nobody ever remembered to give her a present.

That is what Tosca longed for – a Christmas present of her own.

She looked up at the glittering Christmas tree and saw, poised upon the very top, a fairy. Perhaps the fairy would grant her wish for a present.

Tosca waited until she was alone and then started to climb the tree. She had almost reached the top when she felt the tree begin to wobble. It swayed for a moment, then WHOOSH, down it came with a crash of glass balls, a swish of tinsel and a clatter of coloured lights. And down came Tosca.

"Get out, Tosca! You naughty cat!"

Tosca ran into the garden. It was dark and cold. There was snow on the ground and a big moon in the sky. She pressed her nose against the window of the house. It looked very cosy inside. Tosca hoped that they would let her back in. She scratched at the glass, but everyone was too busy and too excited to think about Tosca.

The snowman was not a very comforting companion.

Tosca sat on the lawn and looked up at the sky and watched the stars twinkle. After a long while she seemed to hear the distant tinkling of bells. Something bright and glowing passed high above her in the night sky.

As Tosca watched, the light drew nearer and nearer. The jingle of bells was quite loud now, and Tosca could see a gilded sleigh, drawn by majestic beasts with vast antlers and driven by a plump, white-bearded man in a warm red suit. It was Father Christmas!

Tosca leapt to the roof as the sleigh drew to a halt.

Father Christmas looked so friendly that Tosca approached him with a bold step, and rubbed herself against his boots.

"Hello there, pusscat," said Father Christmas. "You must be cold out here. Wouldn't you be happier back inside?"

"Purrup, purrup," said Tosca.

Tosca was very grateful to Father Christmas for giving her a ride down the chimney in his sack, but she was too shy to ask him whether he had brought anything for her.

As Father Christmas sat by the fire, enjoying the mince pies that had been left for him, Tosca climbed on to his lap. It was very large and very warm. Father Christmas stroked her. Tosca snuggled down, happy and rather drowsy. She had, after all, missed her nap. Her eyes closed and she fell fast asleep . . .

Next morning Tosca woke up by the fireside. Last night's embers were still warm, and from the mantle hung five stockings. One of them was rather smaller than the others. It was embroidered with a large cat.

Tosca thought she must be dreaming. A stocking of her own! She tweaked her whiskers to make sure she was awake.

Then she knocked down her stocking and reached inside it. There was something quite heavy, and it was wrapped up in patterned paper.

Tosca tore at the wrapping with her claws. Her present came tumbling out.

It was a clockwork mouse.

And the card read
**HAPPY  CHRISTMAS,  TOSCA!**